This Little Tiger book belongs to:

_____

_____

_____

For Niki and Nelli – N L

For Noah, Levi, Isaac, Daniel, Dylan and Jacob xxxxxx – J C

LITTLE TIGER PRESS
1 The Coda Centre, 189 Munster Road,
London SW6 6AW
www.littletiger.co.uk
First published in Great Britain 2011
This edition published 2016
Text copyright © Norbert Landa 2011
Illustrations copyright © Jane Chapman 2011
Visit Jane Chapman at www.ChapmanandWarnes.com
Norbert Landa and Jane Chapman have asserted their rights to be
identified as the author and illustrator of this work under the
Copyright, Designs and Patents Act, 1988
All rights reserved
ISBN 978-1-84869-522-1
Printed in China

2 4 6 8 10 9 7 5 3 1

The Slurpy Burpy Bear

Norbert Landa

Jane Chapman

LITTLE TIGER PRESS
London

Big Bear noisily slurped his mushroom stew. He happily chomped and burped. "It's good to be the One and Only Bear!" he thought. "I can eat the way I like!"

CRUNCH! CHOMP! BURP

Across the river Little Rabbit's ears twitched. What was that terrible, crunching, roaring sound?

"Hush!" Mama Rabbit whispered. "That is the Beast's horrible sound!"

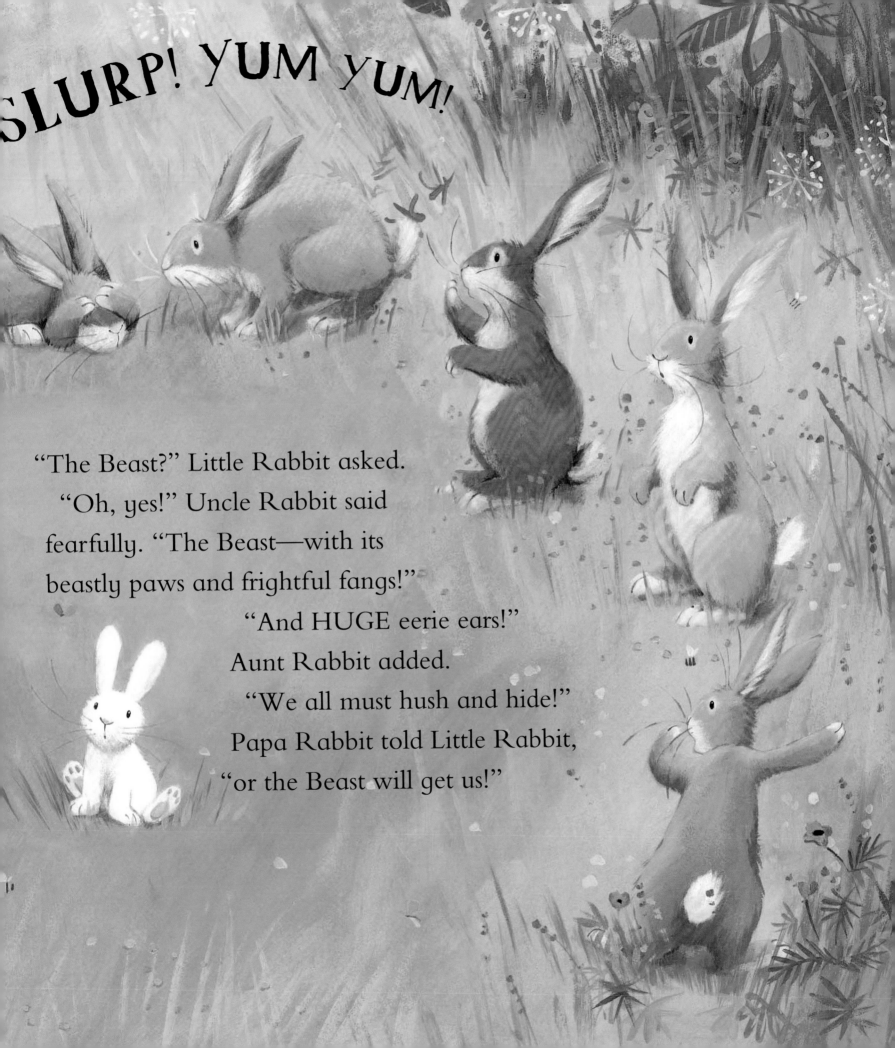

SLURP! YUM YUM!

"The Beast?" Little Rabbit asked.
"Oh, yes!" Uncle Rabbit said
fearfully. "The Beast—with its
beastly paws and frightful fangs!"
"And HUGE eerie ears!"
Aunt Rabbit added.
"We all must hush and hide!"
Papa Rabbit told Little Rabbit,
"or the Beast will get us!"

Big Bear gulped down his
honey and had a last, big burp.
And as he got up, his bottom le
out a trumpy tune. Ooops!

Paaaaa

"The Beast is roaring! Hide, Little Rabbit!" Papa Rabbit shrieked. "And hold your breath—or you may faint from the Beast's bad smell!"

Trembling, the rabbits hid in their burrow.

arp!

Sometimes Big Bear thought of crossing the river to look for a friend. But he dipped his toes in the cold water and shivered. "Brrrr, brrrr, no way!"

Then he sang:

"I am the One and Only,
The One and Only
Lonely Bear,
With no one there
for me to care . . ."

And Big Bear couldn't help crying a little aloud.

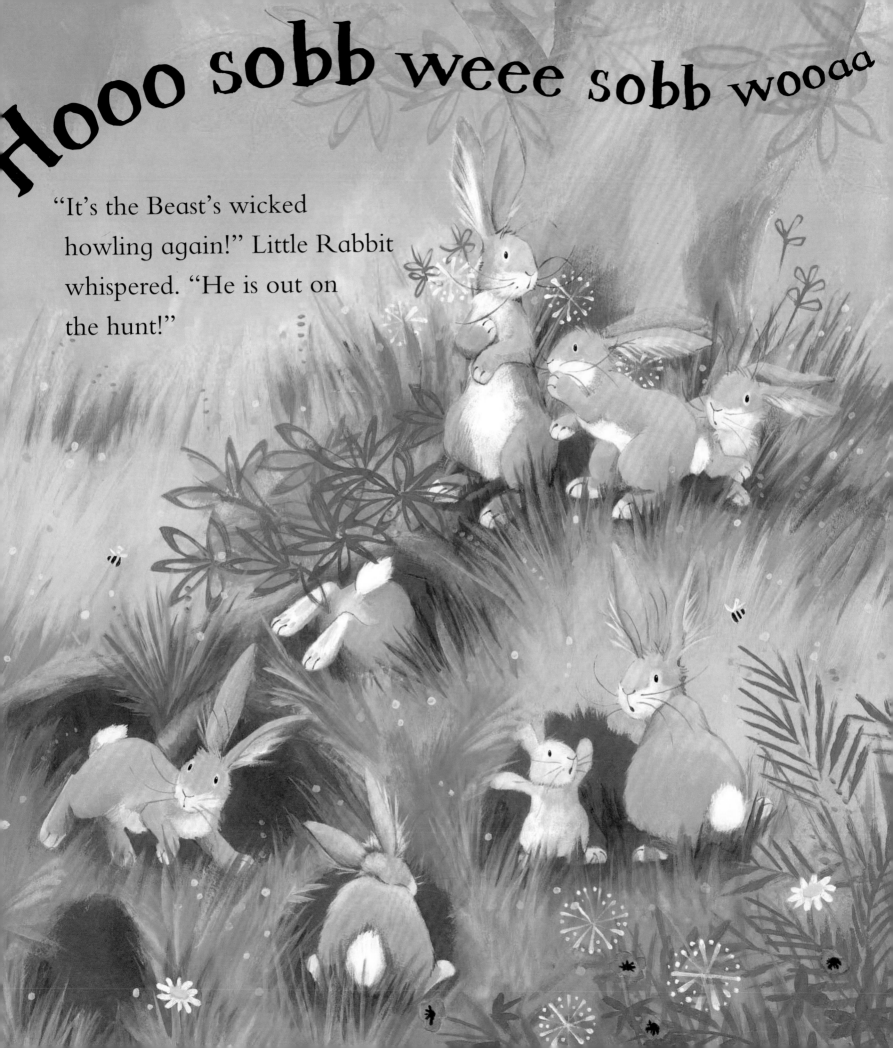

Hooo sobb weee sobb wooaa

"It's the Beast's wicked howling again!" Little Rabbit whispered. "He is out on the hunt!"

One day, as Big Bear scratched against a big, old tree . . .

SNAP!

Snap! the tree cracked and fell across the river.

"I've built a bridge!" Big Bear said proudly. "Now I can look for a friend!" He brushed his fur and set off.

Across the river, Little Rabbit
chased butterflies in the woods.
"You'd better hide!" Little
Rabbit roared, "for I'm the Beast!"
Then suddenly . . .

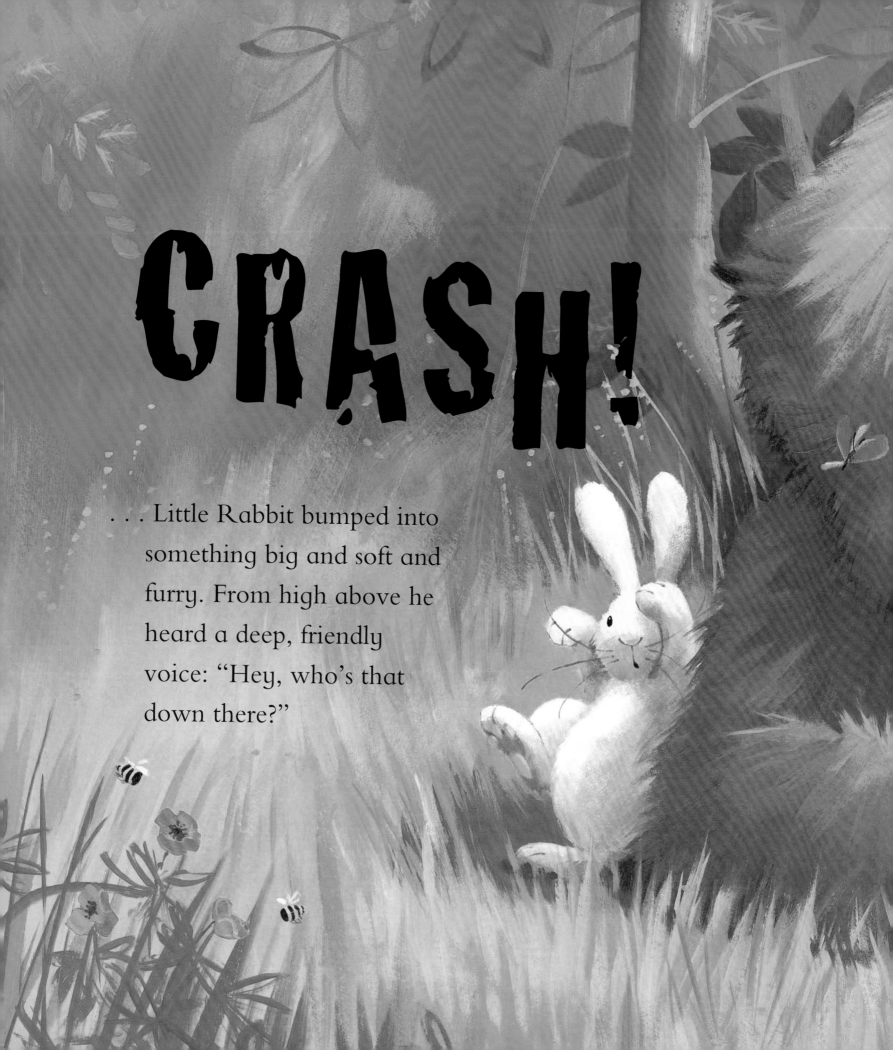

CRASH!

. . . Little Rabbit bumped into something big and soft and furry. From high above he heard a deep, friendly voice: "Hey, who's that down there?"

"I'm Little Rabbit,"
Little Rabbit said as strong
arms lifted him up.
"Oh, my! You are so big!"
"That's because I am Big Bear,"
Big Bear smiled. "Are there more
of you here?"
"Oh, yes!" Little Rabbit said.
"But we always hide from the Beast!"
"Beast?" Big Bear asked. "What Beast?"

Little Rabbit told Big Bear all about
the Beast's

roaring and howling and frightful fangs

and bad smell.

"Well, I've never seen any Beast,"
Big Bear said. "Perhaps I
could protect you."
"Oh, yes, please!"
Little Rabbit cheered.

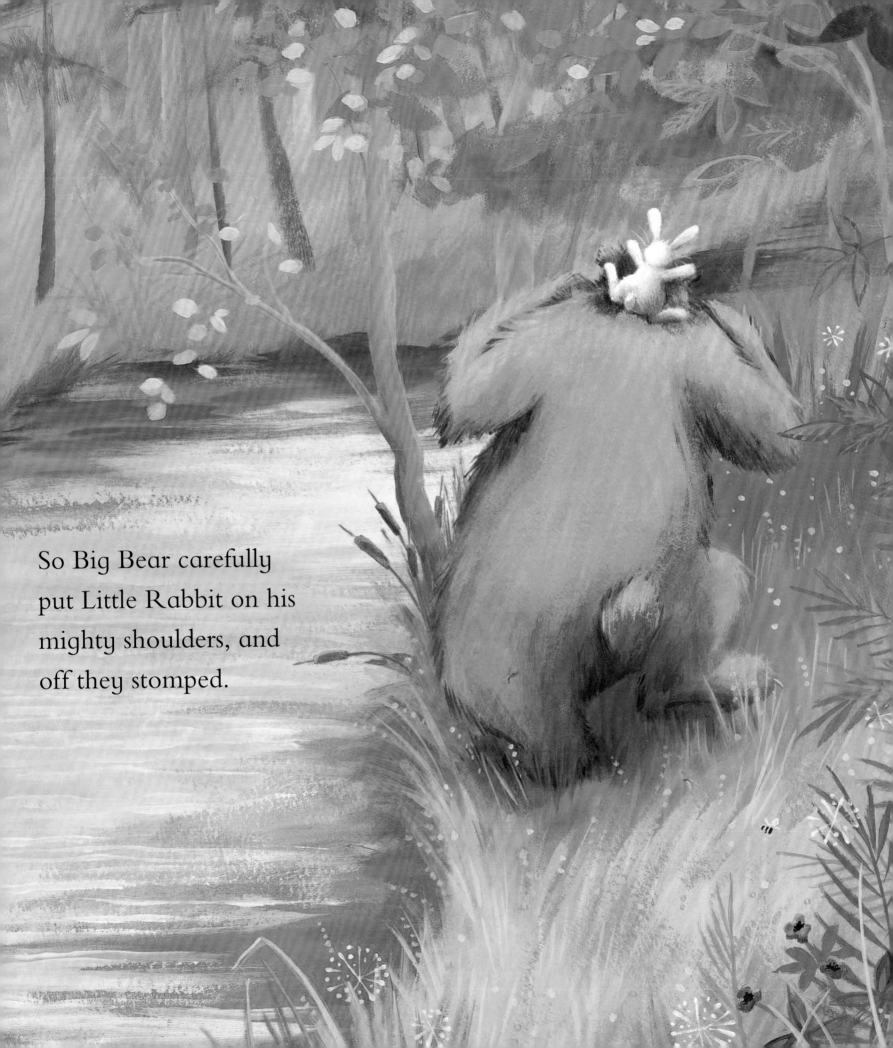

So Big Bear carefully put Little Rabbit on his mighty shoulders, and off they stomped.

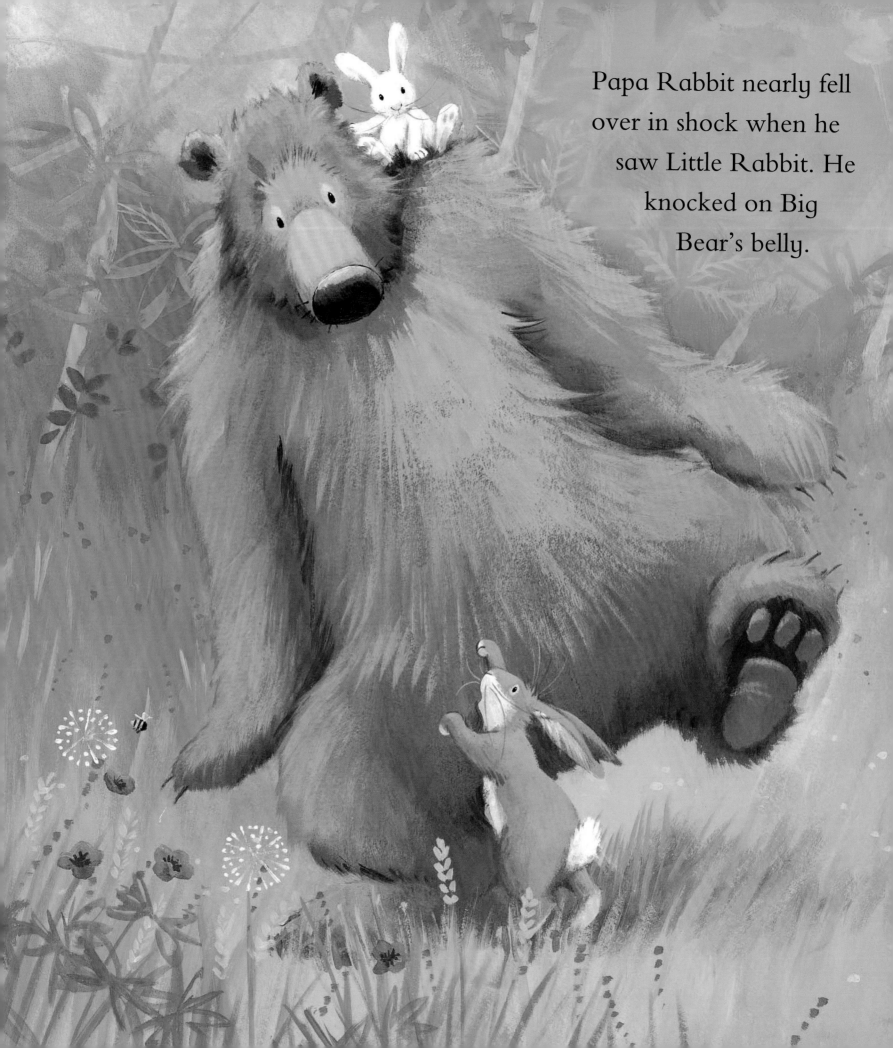

Papa Rabbit nearly fell over in shock when he saw Little Rabbit. He knocked on Big Bear's belly.

"Don't you do Little Rabbit any
   harm!" he cried.
   "Don't worry, Papa!" Little Rabbit called.
"Big Bear is my friend. He has promised
   to protect us from the Beast!"

"Can you really protect us?" Mama Rabbit asked.

"Yes, I can!" Big Bear answered with a smile. He let everyone feel his muscles and sit on his paws.

"Stay with us, Big Bear!" the rabbits cheered.

So Big Bear stayed, and soon the rabbits forgot all about the Beast. Only sometimes, faint sounds reminded them of something . . .

"You must never do this with others around you," Big Bear whispered to Little Rabbit.

And they giggled together.

SLURP! SLURP! BURP!

As for Big Bear . . .

. . . he was so happy to no longer be
the One and Only Lonely Bear.
  And when it was time to sleep,
he snuggled up with the rabbits and
sang to himself:
  "I am no longer lonely,
  I am the Only
  Big and Happy Bear.
  My little friends may
  slumber safe and sound,
  Because they know
  I'm always there."